SQUARE CAT

FOR JOHN,
MACKENZIE
& SAYWARD
X O X O X O

ALADDIN • An imprint of Simon & Schuster Children's Publishing Division • 1230 Avenue of the Americas, New York, NY 10020 • First Aladdin hardcover edition January 2011 • Copyright © 2011 by Elizabeth Schoonmaker • All rights reserved, including the right of reproduction in whole or in part in any form. • ALADDIN is a trademark of Simon & Schuster, Inc., and related logo is a registered trademark of Simon & Schuster, Inc. • For information about special discounts for bulk purchases, please contact Simon & Schuster Special Sales at 1-866-506-1949 or business@simonandschuster.com. • The Simon & Schuster Speakers Bureau can bring authors to your live event. For more information or to book an event contact the Simon & Schuster Speakers Bureau at 1-866-248-3049 or visit our website at www.simonspeakers.com. • Designed by Karin Paprocki • The text of this book was set in Museo. • The illustrations for this book were rendered in watercolor. • Manufactured in China • 1010 SCP • 10 9 8 7 6 5 4 3 2 1 • Library of Congress Cataloging-in-Publication Data • Schoonmaker, Elizabeth. • Square cat / written and illustrated by Elizabeth Schoonmaker. — 1st Aladdin hardcover ed. • p. cm. • Summary: Eula the cat is square and, while she longs to be round like other cats, her friends show her the benefits of the shape that she has. • ISBN 978-1-4424-0619-3 (hardcover) • [1. Individuality—Fiction. 2. Self-acceptance—Fiction. 3. Shape—Fiction. 4. Cats—Fiction.] I. Title. • PZ7.S3763Sq 2011 • [E]—dc22 • 2009039884

SQUARE CAT

Written and illustrated by

Elizabeth Schoonmaker

ALADDIN

NEW YORK   LONDON   TORONTO   SYDNEY

Eula was a square cat.

She longed to be a round cat
like her friends Patsy and Maude.
But Eula was square.

Life wasn't easy for a square cat.

Mouse holes were impossible.

And when Eula tipped over,
it was hard to get back up.

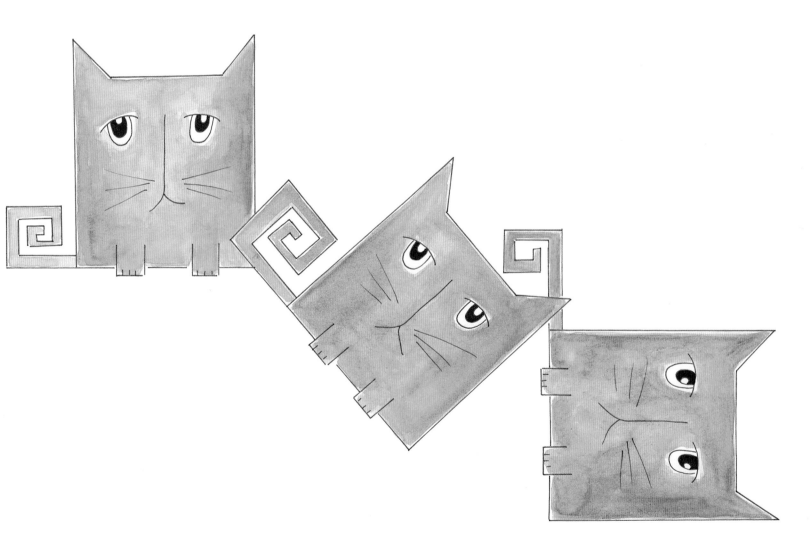

Eula was invisible in a city.

And her favorite circle skirt
didn't quite fit right.

Red shoes made her look short.

And stripes were just plain wrong . . .
up and down or back and forth.

Eula was unhappy as a square cat.
So unhappy that she lost her purr.

Patsy and Maude tried to make Eula feel round.
They gave her hoop earrings
and a beehive hat.

Patsy painted a red rouge circle
on one of Eula's cheeks.

Maude painted the other cheek.

All together, Patsy, Maude, and Eula rounded
their lips and sang, "Ooooooooooooo . . ."
while they skipped in circles,
eating doughnuts.

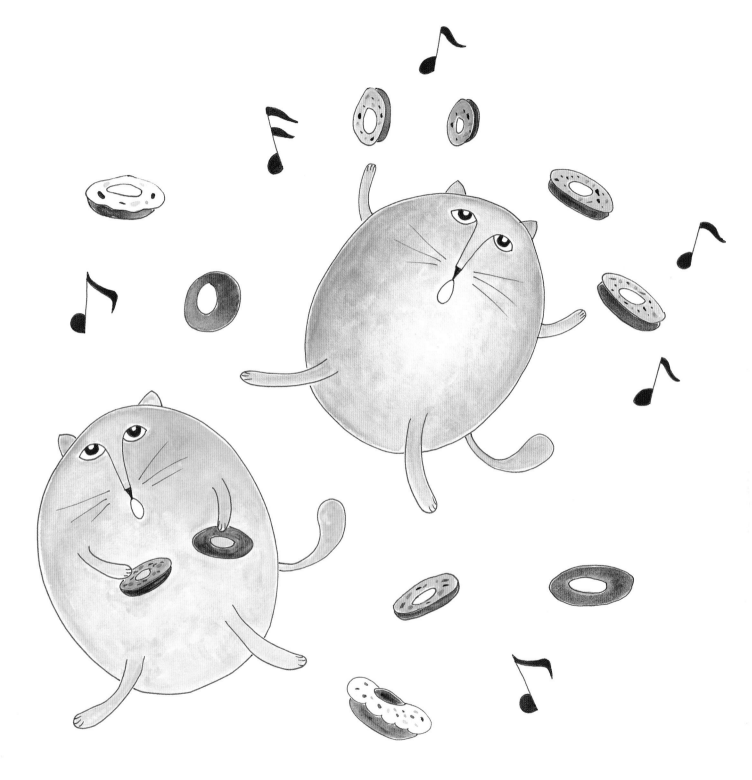

Eula began to feel round,
until she tripped and tipped over,

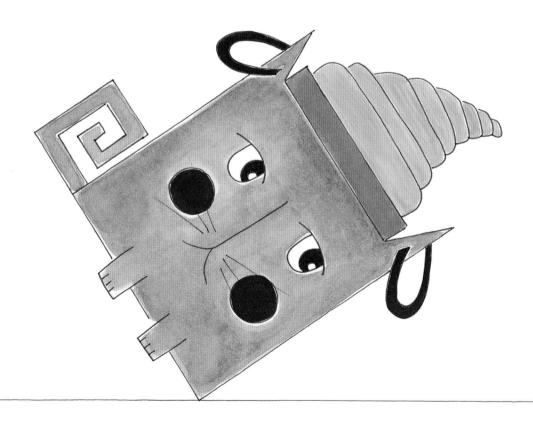

which, as you know, is not good
for a square cat.

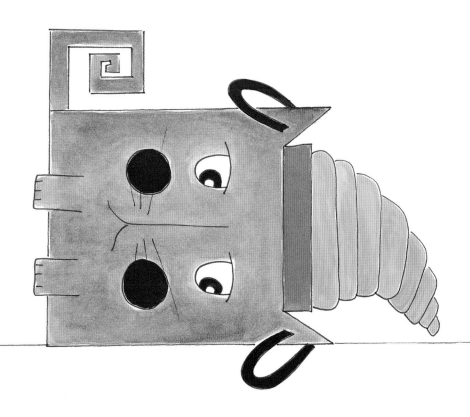

That gave Patsy and Maude an idea.
They each slipped into a box.

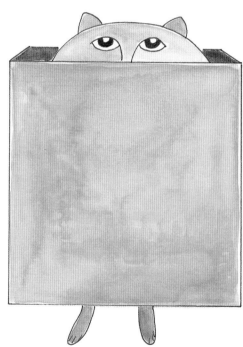

They became square cats,
just like Eula.

They showed Eula that a checkerboard sweater with a pillbox hat look dazzling on a square cat . . .

and how a painting of a square cat
is priceless.

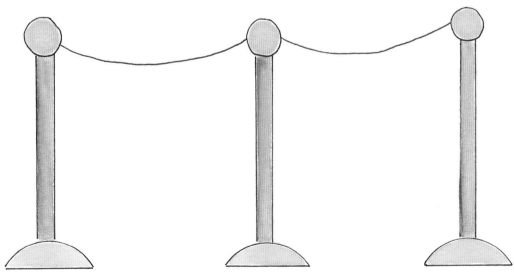

As for mouse holes . . .
they are impossible for all cats,
round or square.

Eula was surprised.
She didn't know that.

Patsy and Maude showed Eula that
square cats are easy to stack,

are natural
billboards,

and are excellent square dancers.

Eula jumped with joy . . .
tipped . . . and got stuck, like always.

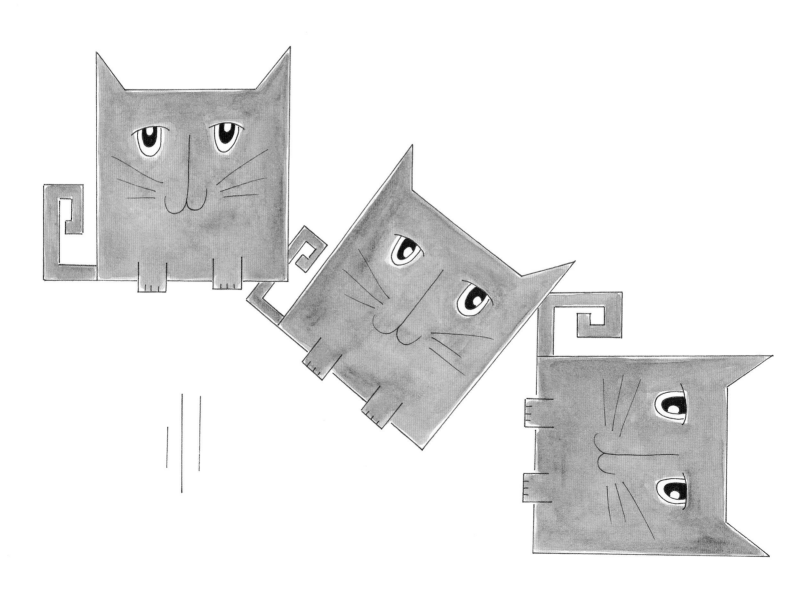

Patsy and Maude jumped and tipped too ...
and got stuck next to Eula.

Stuck flat on their square backs,
the three cats gazed into the blue sky.
Only a square cat could have this view.
Eula purred. Patsy and Maude smiled.